# Creta
## The Winged Terror

Creta the Winged Terror was originally
published as a Beast Quest special. This
version has been specially adapted for
developing readers.

*You will earn one special gold coin for every chapter*
*you* 840000049290 *to do with your*

With special thanks to Lucy Courtenay
and Fiona Munro

Reading Consultant: Prue Goodwin, lecturer in literacy and
children's books

ORCHARD BOOKS
Carmelite House
50 Victoria Embankment
London EC4Y 0DZ

*Creta the Winged Terror* first published in 2010
This Early Reader edition published in 2015
Text © Beast Quest Limited 2010, 2015
Cover and inside illustrations by Steve Sims © Beast Quest Limited 2010, 2015

A CIP catalogue record for this book is available from the British Library.

ISBN 978 1 40833 924 4

Printed in China

The paper and board used in this book are made from wood
from responsible sources.

Orchard Books
An imprint of Hachette Children's Group
Part of The Watts Publishing Group Limited
An Hachette UK Company

www.hachette.co.uk
www.beastquest.co.uk

# Creta
## The Winged Terror

## BY ADAM BLADE

ORCHARD

# Beasts of Avantia

THE PIT OF FIRE

MALVEL'S MAZE

STONEWIN VOLCANO

THE DEAD VALLEY

THE DEAD JUNGLE

ERRINEL

THE DARKWOOD

THE DARK JUNGLE

# CONTENTS

STORY ONE

# THE DEADLY SWARM

An ancient curse is on its way to Avantia and the evil Malvel is behind it.

Thank goodness we have a hero, Tom, son of Taladon, to face such magic.

# Chapter 1

# The Swarm

Tom felt happy as he stared up at a sky full of stars. He was camping in the mountains with his father, Taladon, who was Avantia's Master of Beasts.

It was a humid night and as Tom wiped his forehead he felt something crawling on his skin. Brushing it off, he could see it was some kind of cockroach, its black shell gleaming in the moonlight. "Urgh!" he

exclaimed, watching it fly
away. Then Tom let out a
gasp – the ground was
crawling with insects, some
creeping on the sleeping
Taladon. Tom jumped to his
feet, waking his father.

"What are they?" Tom asked as the stinking black-shelled creatures scuttled around his feet.

"I don't know," his father replied, puzzled, as the swarm skimmed close to their heads and were gone.

Something about the insects unsettled Tom, but after a few moments he and his father settled back down beside the fire. The smoke seemed to be moving...taking shape...

Tom's eyes widened. There was the face of his friend Elenna, who, together with her wolf, Silver, had accompanied him on his Quests. She looked worried.

"Avantia is suffering from an infestation of some kind of bug," she said. "The kingdom needs your help!"

At first light, Tom and Taladon galloped up to King Hugo's castle. Even though it was dawn, it already felt as hot as midday. Something was terribly wrong.

The stinking air was black with insects. As their horses,

Storm and Fleetfoot, drank at a water trough, Tom noticed the castle walls were being eaten away by insects.

Tom banged on the door. A small window slid open and a pair of terrified eyes gazed out at them.

"The swarm," whispered the sentry, recognising Tom and Taladon. "It's eating everything it can find."

"Let us in!" Tom demanded. "We need to see King Hugo immediately."

Tom and Taladon raced up the stone steps and burst into the throne room where Aduro, the king's wizard, rose to greet them. Elenna was there too.

"Welcome," said King Hugo grimly as Tom and Taladon watched precious tapestries being eaten by the bugs that swarmed over them.

"They are Stabiors," explained Elenna.

"But Stabiors left Avantia years ago!" Taladon said.

"Well, they're back," said

Aduro soberly.

"Malvel," Tom guessed. "Is that who's done this?"

Everyone fell silent at the mention of the evil sorceror's name.

*Creeaakk!* They watched from the window as a huge tower, black with insects, crumbled to the ground before them.

1

# Chapter 2

# Insect Armour

Tom hurtled outside to the courtyard, where the rubble of the collapsed tower was settling. People limped past with gashes on their arms and legs.

"Captain Harkman has disappeared!" shouted a sentry, running through the dust. The captain was the commander of King Hugo's troops.

Tom shuddered. If the captain

had been hit by the falling
tower, it was almost certain that
he was dead. As they searched
through the rubble, clouds of
Stabiors flew in black clouds.

Tom and Taladon hurried
into the castle in case Harkman
had taken refuge inside.

Rushing through the castle, Tom and Taladon eventually came up against a locked door. "This is where the magical Golden Armour is kept!" Tom exclaimed.

They rammed their shoulders at the door until it broke from its hinges. There was no sign of Captain Harkman, but the Golden Armour had gone and the Master-of-Arms lay injured.

"The Stabiors," he gasped. "They carried pieces of the armour away. They crawled all over me! This breastplate is all that is left!"

"Malvel," said Taladon softly.

Tom felt a wave of anger break over him. "He won't get away with this," he vowed.

Back in the throne room, Tom noticed one of the magical tokens was glowing on his shield. It was Epos's talon. Epos was one of Avantia's six great Beasts – a huge phoenix who lived in the Stonewin Volcano. She must need him.

As Tom explained to the king that he had to go, Aduro spoke. "Follow me," he said, leading Tom and Elenna to a secret room, deep beneath the castle.

Four suits of armour rested on stands. Tom reached out and

touched the nearest breastplate.

"Stabiors!" he gasped, pulling his hand away.

"Stabior *shells*," said Aduro. "Woven into suits of armour. They resist and reflect heat," Aduro explained. "I think you will find this armour useful on your Quest."

# Chapter 3

# Epos in Trouble

Tom and Elenna felt cool
in their new armour as they
galloped across the hot ground
on Storm, with Elenna's wolf,

Silver, running alongside.
The Stonewin Volcano was
on the horizon, but it wasn't
heat making it shimmer,
Tom realised. *It's a vast cloud
of Stabiors!* As the ground
became more difficult, they left
the animals in the village of
Rokwin, and continued on foot.
The heat increased as they went
higher. Their armour was the
only thing keeping them alive.
They walked quickly, the cloud
of Stabiors and the outline of
Epos the phoenix above them.

At the barren crown of the
volcano, Epos lay on her side
amongst a mass of smashed
boulders.

"She's been injured," Elenna

gasped. "There must have been a rock fall!"

Making their way quickly up the final stretch of the mountain path, Tom rushed to Epos's side. The phoenix's eyes were clouded with pain and her plumage had lost its fiery colour. At once, Tom and Elenna pulled away the rocks, the Stabiors buzzing madly around them, until with a mighty screech of joy, the phoenix raised both her wings and flew up into the sky.

Tom struggled up closer to the volcano to see that instead of fire, broken rocks filled the crater. Those Stabiors that had survived the rock fall were busy eating away the edge of the crater. Tom realised they had blocked the volcano on purpose!

"No wonder the kingdom is warming up," said Elenna, standing beside him.

"The heat needs to escape somehow, or there's going to be..." said Tom slowly.

*BOOOOM!*

Tom and Elenna were thrown to the ground as boiling rocks rained down.

"The lava!" Tom gasped, lifting his head to watch a snake of red pour down the mountain, straight towards the village.

Tom jumped to his feet. They had to outpace the lava and warn the village, but the lava was so fast. He slid and scrambled down the mountainside. Elenna ran close beside him, her armour glittering. Epos wheeled and screeched overhead. Tom threw himself at a large rock and tried to push it into the path of the lava.

"If we can divert the flow, we can save Rokwin!" he shouted to Elenna. They pushed

desperately, but they weren't
strong enough. The boulder
didn't move. "Get down to the
village!" Tom said to Elenna.
"Start evacuating the people!
Everyone must leave!"

1

# Chapter 4

# The Captain Returns

Who could Tom turn to for help?
The answer came to him as he
stared at the precious tokens on
his shield. *Arcta! The mountain
giant. Of course!*

Quickly, Tom rubbed the eagle
feather that Arcta had given him,
then scanned the horizon. First,
he heard booming steps, then he
saw Arcta's shaggy head rising
above the mountains.

"Arcta!" Tom cried, delighted to see his old friend. "Throw!"

Arcta scooped up an armful of huge rocks and flung them into the lava. Slowly, the boiling river began to change direction. The people of Rokwin were safe.

Down in the village again, a thundercloud of Stabiors appeared from nowhere. Tom gazed up as the insects twisted and moved. Deep in their midst a face took shape – the face of Malvel.

"Until you meet Creta," echoed his booming voice, "you know nothing of the terror that awaits you."

Tom unsheathed his sword. "I've fought you before, Malvel, and I'll fight you again," he threatened bravely.

Malvel vanished, but the Stabiors re-formed into a vast column, sprouting arms and a terrifying face. A pair of huge orange eyes, with pupils like black lightning, gazed at Tom.

Tom knew this dreadful Beast was Creta.

As the giant Beast advanced, Tom saw that several pieces of the Golden Armour glinted on its limbs. He leapt back in shock as the creature leaned towards him and opened its mouth. A second face lurked inside Creta's mouth. It was a human face twisted in pain, with eyes full of terror.

It was Captain Harkman.

"Help!" the captain cried in desperation as insects crawled across his face.

Tom suddenly realised what

must have happened at the
castle. Malvel's swarm had
kidnapped the captain and
trapped him inside this Beast.
An unbeatable monster, made
from the bodies of a hundred
thousand insects.

1

# STORY TWO

# WATER OF LIFE

Poor Captain Harkman – now at the mercy of Malvel's swarm. Have Tom and his faithful companions enough courage to overcome Creta and rescue the captain? Or will this be one challenge too many for Taladon's son?

# Chapter 1

# Creta

Staring at the monstrous Beast that stood in front of him, Tom knew this would be a tough Quest. How could he fight a monster like Creta and save Captain Harkman? Arcta was still standing beside him in the village square, his gigantic feet planted like trees on either side of Rokwin's pond. He roared and swiped at Creta with fists like boulders, leaving a small hole in Creta's side. The Stabiors scattered to avoid the Beast's attack. Arcta's head disappeared in a cloud of black wings as he staggered from side to side, while the hideous creatures clawed at his face.

"Distract him, Elenna!" Tom called, before watching with despair as the swarm slid away from her arrows and began to change shape. Its front legs were now growing longer and more pointed. The tips divided and curled to form pincers that slashed the air. With his sword, Tom managed to shatter one. To his dismay, it immediately began to re-form. He threw himself towards the Beast again, whirling his sword to break up the swarm of Stabiors

and brushing them off his
armour. He couldn't let them
seize him in the way they had
taken Captain Harkman.

Tom could feel the Stabiors marching up his neck, digging hard into his skin. They were in his hair and tickling his ears

but he had no time to push them away because Creta's pincers were slashing all around him. Suddenly Tom felt a stinging pain deep in his head. He dropped his sword and fell to his knees.

The voice, when it came, was icy cold as it boomed through Tom's head.

*Now I have you!*

Malvel's next words chilled Tom to the bone.

*What can you do to defeat me, now that I am inside your head?*

Tom shook his head. Malvel's laughter felt like poison.

"Look out!" Elenna screamed as, just in time, Tom rolled away from Creta's swarming pincer. He stumbled to his feet as a great shriek rang through the air. It was Epos, her magnificent red wings spread wide.

"Get back, Elenna!" Tom warned as the phoenix's attack took Creta by surprise. As Epos's great wings tore through its body, Stabiors were scattered

in all directions. This time the
swarm-Beast had no chance to
rebuild itself. The buzzing black
cloud broke apart and drifted
back towards the village. Creta
was defeated – for now.

Tom could feel Malvel's laughter fading, but he clutched his stomach as he felt a stabbing pain deep in his guts. He fell, and everything went black.

Opening his eyes much later, Tom found himself back at the castle, Elenna by his bedside. She must have brought him back somehow. All at once, memories rushed at Tom. He closed his eyes in shame as he remembered how Creta had defeated him.

*Yes*, Malvel hissed in his head. *You have failed, Tom.*

Tom pressed his hands against the sides of his head, trying to force the voice away.

# Chapter 2

# The Only Hope

"What is wrong with me, Elenna?" Tom asked.

"I can answer that," said a
voice from a dark corner.

Tom hadn't noticed Marc
sitting in the shadows, a book
in his lap.

"I found this volume in Aduro's library," he said. "It mentions a plague similar to this one."

"How can the bugs be stopped?" asked Tom, feeling desperate.

"There is a spring high in the Shadow Mountains," Marc began. "Its water contains a powerful magic."

With an almighty effort, Tom swung his legs out of the bed. "Tell me how to get there," he said.

The young wizard stood up. "Before you begin this Quest, you need to know what's happened to you," he said grimly. "The Stabiors have laid their eggs inside you, Tom. If you don't drink some of the spring water yourself, you'll soon be under the Beast's control," Marc explained. "My magic will help you get there, but the rest is up to you."

Marc chanted a spell and the bedchamber began to swirl. When the mists cleared, Tom

and Elenna found themselves
in a strange, grey, foggy world,
and in front of them was a
giant waterfall crashing into a
deep foaming pool.

Tom, groaning in pain, moved slowly towards the waterfall after Elenna. The fog was thickening and the waterall kept disappearing from view.

"I'll carry your shield," Elenna suggested, lifting it gently from Tom's back.

Suddenly, a foul smell hit Tom's senses. Creta was back. Twisting round, Tom saw a great pincer rushing towards him, and rolled away just in time.

"Elenna," he croaked as

Creta lifted his evil head, black eyes looming.

Suddenly Creta stumbled, and split in half as Elenna flung Tom's shield at the monster. The Stabiors swarmed, then flew away among the rocks.

# Chapter 3

# The Shadow Mountains

Tom crawled towards his shield and fastened it safely onto his back. "Creta will return," he said. "We have to keep going."

The waterfall and its pool taunted them, flickering in and out of sight in the mist.

The next time Creta appeared, Tom was ready. He slammed his shield into Creta's chest, the only part unprotected

by the Golden Armour. Creta
roared with pain as one huge
foot entered the foaming river.
A glint of hope surged through
Tom. "If we can get the Beast
into the pool, the battle will be
won," he shouted to Elenna.

Tom was in such pain now, he was crawling along on his knees. For safety, they stayed close to the river, as Creta was keeping a wary distance from its glittery depths.

Just ahead of him, Tom watched as Elenna slipped and fell into a marshy pool. The water sucked hungrily at her as she struggled.

"Don't," Tom mumbled. "Struggling makes it worse..."

Panting, he crawled closer and Elenna seized his hand.

Despite the pain, Tom dragged her free, Stabiors dive-bombing them from all directions.

"We're nearly there, Tom," Elenna said to him. "Then you must drink."

Courage pushed him onwards.

As the spray of the waterfall touched Tom's face, he lifted his head and opened his eyes. He crawled to a ledge at the very base of the falls as Stabiors swarmed overhead, afraid to come too close to the water. Tom pulled himself onto the ledge and let the water pound down on him. He rolled onto his back and opened his mouth. Tom felt the water's cleansing power as Malvel screamed from within him in fury. As magic coursed through Tom's body,

the pain and burning ceased.

The curse was gone.

Tom sprang to his feet, feeling more alive than he could ever remember. Down by the edge of the pool, he could see Elenna fighting off the Stabiors. Creta prowled around the far side of the pool, grunting with rage.

Tom saw it could come no closer. The waterfall spray burned it like fire. He thrust his sword into the cascading water, then jumped down from the ledge, his sword dripping magical water.

Striding towards Creta, Tom taunted the Beast.

"Scared of water, are you?" he said. But Creta moved like lightning, its pincers crashing towards him.

# Chapter 4
# The End of the Beast

Tom quickly darted out of the way, magical water dripping from his sword.

Jabbing wildly at the Beast, at last Tom felt his sword connect with the Stabiors. Bugs rained down, hissing gently as

the water burned them away
to nothing. Elenna cheered
as Creta staggered. One of its
pincers was broken into pieces.
Tom dropped down and dipped
the sword in the water again.

"Look out, Tom!" Elenna
screamed suddenly.

Whirling round, Tom stabbed
instinctively with his sword.
Creta the Winged Terror was
right behind him, but now it
was staggering again.

This time Tom had stabbed
the Beast through the middle.

The tottering Beast keeled
over and fell into the pool.
There was a flash of white fire
as Creta disappeared beneath
the water and a great geyser
erupted, shooting skywards.
Tom and Elenna both heard

a shriek coming from deep beneath the pool's glittering surface before the water settled to stillness. It was the voice of Malvel.

Tom hardly dared hope that they had won.

"They've gone!" Elenna said into the silence.

Tom stepped back as something bubbled and exploded to the surface. It was Captain Harkman, coughing and spluttering, but alive...and wearing the Golden Armour.

"Well done, Tom and Elenna!" came a familiar voice.

Aduro stood smiling on the banks of the pool in a shimmering ring of fire.

"What news of the castle?" asked Elenna anxiously.

"The creatures have gone," said Aduro. "And the king awaits you!"

The wizard waved his wand and they were magically whisked back to the castle. Happy faces met Tom and Elenna everywhere they looked.

"I thank you," said King Hugo warmly, "for driving this fresh peril from our kingdom. Thanks to you, and to young Marc's magic, we are safe again. Let the feasting and celebrating begin!"

1

If you enjoyed this story, you may want to read

# Arax
## The Soul Stealer
### EARLY READER

Here's how the story begins...

Tom and Elenna were staying at the Palace as guests of King Hugo. Sunshine streamed through the windows as the friends ran downstairs. Then

Tom stopped. "What can you hear, Elenna?" he asked.

"Nothing," she replied. "It's really quiet."

"Exactly," said Tom. "We haven't even seen a servant."

The Great Hall lay silent. The king's throne was empty. No fire had been lit.

"It's really spooky," agreed Elenna. Then a guard burst in.

"You there," he said. "I have orders from the king. You must go to the wizard Aduro's chambers straight away."

"Where is everyone?" asked Elenna.

"They are in their rooms, by order of the king. The Palace is not safe," replied the guard.

Tom and Elenna ran up the spiral staircase that led to Aduro's private rooms. The wooden door glowed strangely around the edges.

Inside, the friends found a man with wild eyes, hissing and growling. He was being closely watched by guards.

The man was their old friend,

the good wizard Aduro himself.

Tom stared in horror. Aduro's face, usually filled with kindness, was instead twisted in anger.

READ

# Arax
## The Soul Stealer
**EARLY READER**

TO FIND OUT WHAT HAPPENS NEXT!

# LEARN TO READ WITH

## EARLY READER

Beast Quest Early Readers are easy-to-read versions of the original books

Perfect for parents to read aloud and for newly confident readers to read along

Remember to enjoy reading together. It's never too early to share a story!

# Series 1
# COLLECT THEM ALL!

## Meet Tom, Elenna and the first six Beasts!

**FERNO**
THE FIRE DRAGON

978-1-84616-483-5

**SEPRON**
THE SEA SERPENT

978-1-84616-482-8

**ARCTA**
THE MOUNTAIN GIANT

978-1-84616-484-2

**TAGUS**
THE HORSE MAN

978-1-84616-486-6

**NANOOK**
THE SNOW MONSTER

978-1-84616-485-9

**EPOS**
THE FLAME BIRD

978-1-84616-487-3

# CONGRATULATIONS, YOU HAVE COMPLETED THIS QUEST!

At the end of each chapter you were awarded a special gold coin. The QUEST in this book was worth an amazing **8** coins.

Look at the Beast Quest totem picture inside the back cover of this book to see how far you've come in your journey to become

## MASTER OF THE BEASTS.

The more books you read, the more coins you will collect!

---

*Do you want your own Beast Quest Totem?*

1. Cut out and collect the coin below
2. Go to the Beast Quest website
3. Download and print out your totem
4. Add your coin to the totem

**www.beastquest.co.uk/totem**